The young Queen Arianna, great-granddaughter of King Langilor, now ruled the Kingdom of Lugin. Eleven years had passed since the death of her parents, and the Queen's reign was in danger.

During her youth, the Royal Advisors had overseen the Kingdom. Greedy for more power, they banished all wizards from the Royal City and exiled dragons from the land. With the dragons gone, trolls and monsters began to occupy the forests, and Lugin entered a time of sadness and decay.

Yet, a prophecy engraved upon a sacred stone gave hope to the people:

From the cold of Lugin's night
A wizard child shall reignite
The sacred fire that guards life's well
And heal the land in which we dwell.

"The Little Wizard was inspired by my journey to Ireland, where I rode horseback on the historical Wicklow Trail from Dublin to the sixth century city of Glendalough. Founded by St. Kevin, this famous walled city was an important center of Celtic art for 400 years. Kevin is remembered as a great leader, a visionary, and a worker of miracles.

In his later years, Saint Kevin retreated to a cave overlooking Glenalough's picturesque lake. I was able to spend time there contemplating his extraordinary legacy. This book is dedicated to Saint Kevin and all who embark on the journey to realize their greatest potential."

Jody Bergsma

With appreciation to: John, Ruth and Arrieana Thompson, Andrea Hurst,
Merina Greene, and Lori Robinson from Illumination Arts
for their superb editing assistance.

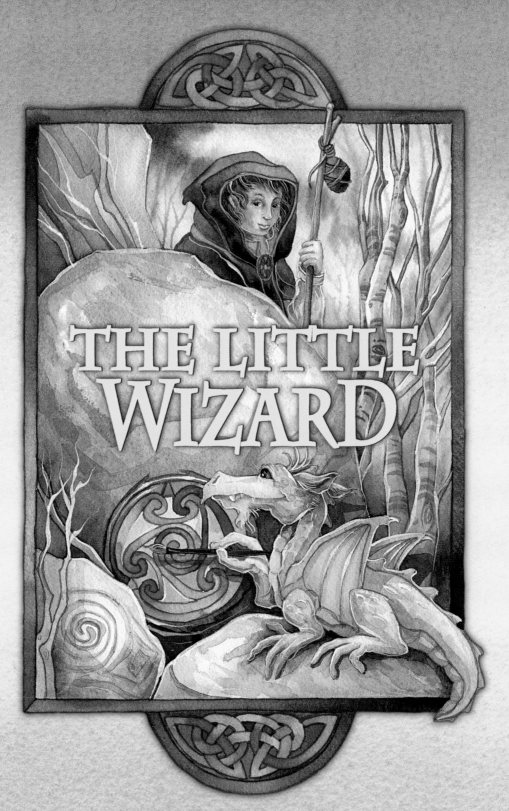

THE LITTLE WIZARD

Written and illustrated by

JODY BERGSMA

ILLUMINATION ARTS PUBLISHING COMPANY, INC.

BELLEVUE, WASHINGTON

Winter Solstice had passed, and the promise of snow hung like a cloak over purple hills. Far from the Royal City, a young boy named Kevin sat with his cat by the fire, while his mother lay quietly in the next room. His grieving father kept watch by her bedside.

Living simple lives, the family had been spared the turmoil felt in other parts of the Kingdom. But now a dark cloud had settled over the cottage – Kevin's mother was gravely ill.

The boy's elderly father shuffled to the fire. "Son, I must ask for your help," he sighed. "Your great-grandfather often spoke of a magic well that is hidden in the Queen's Garden. If you could go there and bring back just one vial of the healing water..."

Kevin's eyes grew wide with astonishment. "Oh, Father, I'm too young to make such a journey alone!"

"You must go," the old man whispered. "This may be your mother's only hope."

3

Despite his fear, Kevin packed a small bag, leaving just enough room for his cat, Tomas. He hugged his parents goodbye, then headed east toward the mountains.

The path led into an enchanted forest where thick, tangled branches hid the sun. Moving through the trees, Kevin heard strange voices whispering, "Go this way... No, go that way." But the sounds came from mischievous trolls, and soon the travelers were lost.

Night began to fall, and the boy shivered in the icy wind. "We must find shelter," he whispered to Tomas.

Just as the first snowflakes swirled to the ground, Kevin found a small cave. He gathered a few branches and attempted to light a fire, but the wood was much too damp. Trying to stay warm, the boy and his cat huddled together in the darkness.

Snow fell throughout the night, and they awoke
to find a fairyland of white. Tomas bounded out to play
in the snow and look for mice, while Kevin searched in vain
for drier wood. Desperate to light a fire, the boy struck his flint
again and again, but to no avail. Then, like a spark in the back
of his mind, he heard his great-grandfather whispering an
ancient chant,

Light, fire, light.
Bring your strength and power.
Come, fire, come.
Dance for me this hour.

Kevin repeated the words, his voice growing louder
and louder with every strike of the flint. Suddenly, the
twigs burst into flames, and a rumbling shook the cave.
Amidst a great shower of sparks, there appeared a
luminous dragon.

"Yieee!" Kevin screeched, as he jumped
back, tripping over his cat.

"W-w-w-where did you c-come from?" stammered the frightened boy.

The dragon stepped out of the flames and bowed politely. "By ancient words, thou hast called me forth to be thy servant. My name is Greystone, after the rocks which gave me birth."

The dragon's friendly manner thawed Kevin's fear, and the splendid fire banished the cold. But something was missing. Where was Tomas?

"Thy cat has run into the forest, Young Master," prompted the dragon.

Kevin followed the paw prints across the snow to the hollow of an old tree, where he found Tomas crouched upon a blue cloth. The boy gently wrapped the cloth around the trembling cat and carried him back to the cave.

Upon seeing Greystone again, Tomas arched his back and hissed. As he leapt away, the woolen cloth flew into the air, landing on Kevin's shoulders. "Why, it's a cloak, and it fits me perfectly!" he said with surprise.

As the chill of the evening settled in, Kevin finally coaxed Tomas into accepting their strange new companion. That night the three travelers happily shared the glowing fire.

In the early morning light, Greystone prepared hot mint tea while Kevin
packed his small bag. "How will I ever find my way through the tangled woods?"
he sighed.

"I would be pleased to be thy guide," pledged the dragon.

"But you can't!" Kevin exclaimed. "Dragons have been banned from Lugin."

"I shall need a disguise, of course," replied Greystone. "Pray give me thine old

cloak. Thou wearest the new one, and we shall be on our way."

Kevin agreed, and together they left for the Royal City. As they traveled through the forest, Greystone instructed the boy in ancient magic. He learned how to disappear in a cloud of smoke and to summon dragon fire. But his favorite lesson was whistling an enchanted tune. Whenever Kevin practiced, Tomas would find himself dancing a merry jig.

Leaving snow and forest behind, the travelers arrived at a small village.
Greystone announced, "Thou must go forth alone, for I cannot be where I am not
respected."

Kevin and Tomas shyly entered the town, hoping to replenish their food
supply. As they passed between the cottages, they could see curious eyes peeking
through the windows. Doors opened and the villagers approached, one by one,

with humble greetings and gifts. One whispered, "Could this be the Promised One?" Another bowed deeply, saying "Welcome, Esteemed One." Others called out, "Hail, Young Master!"

Astonished by the warm welcome, Kevin gratefully accepted gifts of food, clothing, and even a shaggy pony.

When they met Greystone outside the village, Kevin was excited but confused. "What do you think they meant by their bowing – and all these gifts?" he questioned.

"They believe thou art the child wizard spoken of in legend," Greystone replied, "the one who shall restore glorious days to the Kingdom."

"But I'm no wizard," protested the boy.

"I beg to differ, Master," countered the dragon. "By thy fortune, thou wearest a wizard's cloak."

"A wizard's cloak! Why didn't you tell me?" Kevin exclaimed, his voice rising. "I can't wear this! Wizards are banned from the Royal City."

"Remember thy quest, Master," said the dragon. "If thy Queen believes thou art the young wizard foretold in prophecy, she may grant thy request for a vial of the healing water."

Kevin's love for his mother was far stronger than his fear. And so it was that he agreed to journey on, pretending to be the child wizard.

When the travelers reached the next town, Greystone again departed, taking with him the shaggy pony. This time, Kevin and Tomas were given a much different reception. After they entered the city, the gates closed behind them with a resounding clang, and tall guards with sharp spears stepped out from the shadows. Clutching Kevin by his cloak and Tomas by his collar, the guards marched them to the City Square, where a crowd gathered.

They were confronted by a sour-faced official. "How can you be a wizard?" he sneered. "If you truly are the Promised One, prove it!"

As he was pushed onto a small platform, Kevin hoped they wouldn't notice

his legs shaking under his cloak. "Show us your magic," chanted the impatient crowd. "Prove yourself!"

Remembering Greystone's lessons from the forest, Kevin called out, "Working is the bread of life, but dancing is the jam!" Then he started whistling the enchanted tune, and Tomas began to dance – twirling this way and that with great abandon. Soon, everyone joined in, dancing, clapping, spinning, humming. The guards were swaying, and even the officials were tapping their toes.

No one seemed to notice when the little wizard and his dancing cat silently escaped in a puff of magic smoke.

Still trembling, Kevin and Tomas rejoined Greystone and the pony. Fearful of being captured, the travelers slipped away through the forest. Emerging on the third day, they could see the golden towers of the Queen's castle in the early morning sunlight.

"I must go no further," the dragon announced. "Remember, Young Master, thou art what thou believest thyself to be." Then he vanished before their eyes.

Kevin bravely approached the gate, and a guard barked, "Who goes there?"

Summoning his courage, the boy declared, "It is I, Kevin the wizard with Tomas the cat. We have come to see the Queen."

The door creaked open and they entered. As their pony was led away, the travelers were taken before the Royal Advisors. "You, boy! You dare to call yourself a wizard?" scorned the Chief Advisor.

"Yes," Kevin answered bravely.

Looking the boy over from head to toe, another Advisor growled, "Then I suppose you must be taken to the Wizard's Hall as the Queen has ordered."

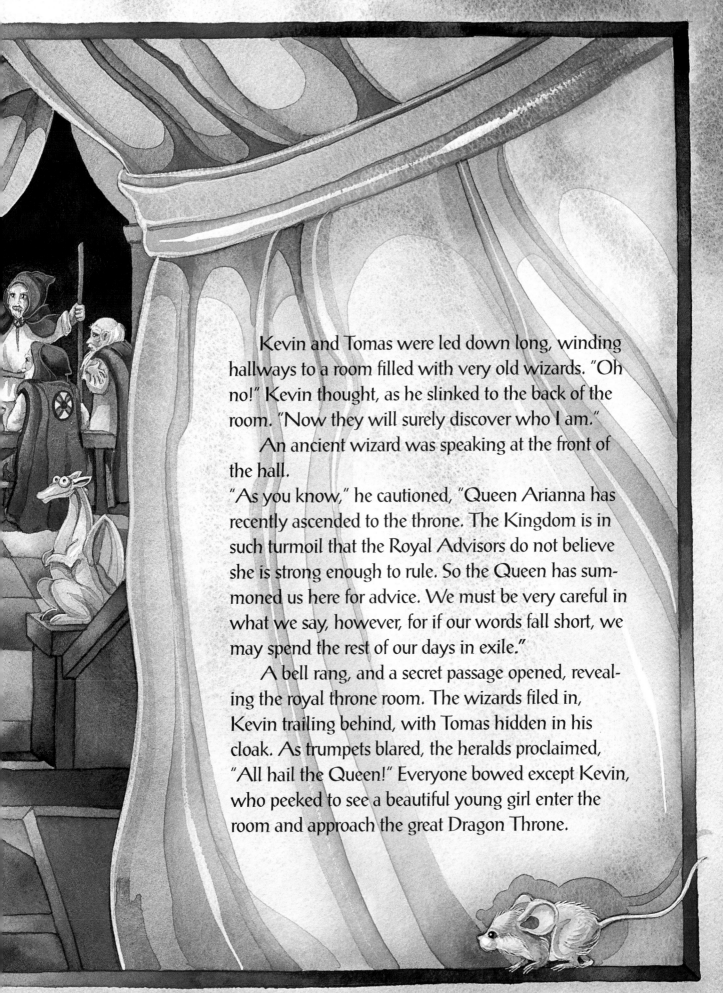

Kevin and Tomas were led down long, winding hallways to a room filled with very old wizards. "Oh no!" Kevin thought, as he slinked to the back of the room. "Now they will surely discover who I am."

An ancient wizard was speaking at the front of the hall.

"As you know," he cautioned, "Queen Arianna has recently ascended to the throne. The Kingdom is in such turmoil that the Royal Advisors do not believe she is strong enough to rule. So the Queen has summoned us here for advice. We must be very careful in what we say, however, for if our words fall short, we may spend the rest of our days in exile."

A bell rang, and a secret passage opened, revealing the royal throne room. The wizards filed in, Kevin trailing behind, with Tomas hidden in his cloak. As trumpets blared, the heralds proclaimed, "All hail the Queen!" Everyone bowed except Kevin, who peeked to see a beautiful young girl enter the room and approach the great Dragon Throne.

With a worried voice, the Queen addressed the gathering: "Clearly, things have not gone well for Lugin since my parents died and wizards were banished from the Royal City. But now I have come of age, and responsibility for the Kingdom is mine. What wisdom can you offer to help bring power to my rule?"

One by one, the wizards came forward. Fearful of angering the court, they chose their words very carefully. Queen Arianna listened, but never smiled, waving each one away. After all the old wizards had spoken, the disappointed Queen scanned the room. "Is there no one else?" she asked.

Kevin was crouching in the back to avoid being seen, when a small gray mouse skittered across the floor. Tomas leapt from under the boy's cloak, and without thinking, he blurted out, "Come back here!"

Everyone turned toward Kevin, including the Queen. "Step forward, Young Wizard," she commanded. "I have not yet heard from you."

The boy felt trapped. His mind went blank and his heart raced as the wizards pushed him toward the throne.

"H - H Hail beautiful Queen," Kevin stammered, trying to gather his thoughts. Suddenly the glowing eyes of the throne dragons caught his attention, and all the teachings of Greystone crystallized in Kevin's mind.

"Your Majesty, there is something I would add to the wizards' wise counsel," he humbly continued. "You and I are both young, and we have many lessons yet to learn. But this one thing I know: To accomplish anything, you must first have a vision and then believe it to be possible. For I have found that for me to be strong I had to trust the power within me."

Kevin paused to take a deep breath. "You are the Kingdom, and the Kingdom is you. You must believe in yourself and your purpose, or you will not succeed."

A loud gasp filled the room, and the faces of the wizards went white. The guards stepped forward to seize the outspoken boy, but Queen Arianna raised her hand. Kevin looked up expecting anger. Instead, a smile of understanding began to light up the Queen's face.

She stood to speak. "This young wizard has been brave enough to tell me what no one else would. He believes in himself, and that is something I had forgotten. His honesty is needed, and his counsel I will accept."

With sighs of relief the audience ended, and everyone began to leave. A troubled Kevin approached the ancient wizard in the hallway and bowed his head. "I must confess something," he said.

But the sage interrupted. "I know what you want to tell me," he smiled, "that you found the cloak by accident and are not a real wizard."

Kevin fell back astonished. "You know about the cloak?"

"How do you think I acquired mine?" the old one chuckled. "You see, for every wizard it is the same. Each one begins a quest and along the way finds a cloak. But choosing to put it on and following° the path that unfolds is not easy. Wearing destiny's cloak requires bravery and commitment. By your courage, you have proven your worthiness to be a wizard, as did your great-grandfather." With a twinkle in his eyes, the ancient wizard turned and walked away.

With renewed confidence, Kevin returned to the throne room and approached the Queen. "Your Majesty, I would be honored to enter your service as you have requested, but something weighs on my heart. My mother lies gravely ill, and only the water from your well can save her."

"I would be most pleased to grant your request," Queen Arianna sighed. "But, alas, the well was magically sealed when the sacred fire died, after dragons were banished from the land. Come, I will show you."

A small group, including the Royal Advisors, gathered around the darkened well. The little wizard closed his eyes and listened for the voice within. Then he began to circle the well, chanting the words that echoed in his mind:

Light, fire, light, open wide this well.
Come, fire, come, break the darkness spell.

A hiss, a crackle, and then a great trembling came from the earth. Amidst a burst of flames, the ancient cover flew open.

Out of the smoky haze came a familiar voice, and Greystone stepped forward. "Thou hast called and the well hath opened. For so long as dragon fire is respected, this flame shall brightly burn."

Still chasing the mouse, Tomas came bounding out of the smoke and tumbled into Kevin and Greystone. Seeing the three sprawled at her feet, the young Queen laughed – and with the sound of her happy laughter, water sprang forth from the well.

As Kevin filled his vial with the sacred water, the Royal Advisors skulked away. Queen Arianna then decreed that dragons and wizards would once again be welcomed throughout the land.

The little wizard prepared for another journey, this time accompanied by Royal Guards. After traveling at great speed to his home, Kevin hurried to his mother's side and gave her the vial of healing water.

She soon recovered, and with grateful hearts they all returned to the Royal City, where Kevin was knighted and became the Queen's most trusted advisor.

So…If thou shall find,
one winter's morn
destiny's cloak,
and it be worn,
be not surprised,
should you achieve
a Wizard's life, if you believe.

P.O. Box 1865, Bellevue, WA 98009
Tel: 425-644-7185 ✣ 888-210-8216 (orders only) ✣ Fax: 425-644-9274
liteinfo@illumin.com ✣ www.illumin.com

✣ ✣

Library of Congress Cataloging-in-Publication Data

Bergsma, Jody.
    The Little Wizard / written and illustrated by Jody Bergsma.
      p cm.
    Summary: A young boy undertakes a perilous quest to save his mother's life. Powerful illustrations weave a mystical spirit throughout this exquisite story.
    ISBN 0-935699-19-8-1
    (1. Wizards Fiction 2. Fantasy.) I. Title
    PZ7B452235 Wz 2000
    (Fic)—wi21
                                                                                    99.25689
                                                                                         CIP

✣ ✣

Published in the United States of America

Printed by Tien Wah Press in Singapore

Book Designer: Molly Murrah, Murrah & Company, Kirkland, Washington

THE ILLUMINATION ARTS COLLECTION OF INSPIRING CHILDREN'S BOOKS

THE DOLL LADY

By H. Elizabeth Collins, illustrated by Judy Kuusisto $15.95   0-935699-24-4

The Doll Lady tells children, "Treat them kindly and with great love, for dolls are just like people."

WINGS OF CHANGE

By Franklin Hill, Ph.D., illlustrated by Aries Cheung. $15.95   0-935699-18-X

A happy little caterpillar learns about his transformation into a butterfly. "As the world turns, so do you. When you change for good, you change the world too."

ALL I SEE IS PART OF ME

By Chara Curtis, illustrated by Cynthia Aldrich. $15.95   0-935699-07-4

Winner – 1996 Award of Excellence from Body Mind Spirit Magazine

An international bestseller. A child finds the light within his heart and his common link with all of life.

THE BONSAI BEAR

Finalist – 2000 Visionary Award for Best Children's Book – Coalition of Visionary Retailers

By Bernard Libster, illustrated by Aries Cheung. $15.95   0-935699-15-5

Issa uses bonsai methods to keep his pet bear small, but the playful cub dreams of following his true nature.

CORNELIUS AND THE DOG STAR

By Diana Spyropulos, illustrated by Ray Williams $15.95   0-935699-08-2

Winner – 1996 Award of Excellence from Body Mind Spirit Magazine

Grouchy old Cornelius Basset Hound can't enter Dog Heaven until he learns about love, fun, and kindness.

DRAGON

Written and Illustrated by Jody Bergsma. $15.95   0-935699-17-1

Winner – 2000 Visionary Award for Best Children's Book – Coalition of Visionary Retailers

Born on the same day, a gentle prince and a fire-breathing dragon share a prophetic destiny.

DREAMBIRDS

By David Ogden, illustrated by Jody Bergsma $16.95   0-935699-09-0

Winner – 1998 Visionary Award for Best Children's Book – Coalition of Visionary Retailers

A Native American boy searches for the elusive dreambird and its powerful gift.

FUN IS A FEELING

By Chara M. Curtis, illustrated by Cynthia Aldrich $15.95   0-935699-13-9

Find your fun! "Fun isn't something or somewhere or who. It's a feeling of joy that lives inside of you."

HOW FAR TO HEAVEN?

By Chara M. Curtis, illustrated by Cynthia Aldrich $15.95   0-935699-06-6

Exploring the wonders of nature, Nanna and her granddaughter discover that heaven is all around us.

THE RIGHT TOUCH

By Sandy Kleven, LCSW, illustrated by Jody Bergsma $15.95   0-935699-10-4

Winner – Benjamin Franklin Parenting Award, Selected as Outstanding by the Parents Council

This beautifully illustrated read-aloud story teaches children how to prevent sexual abuse.

SKY CASTLE

By Sandra Hanken, illustrated by Jody Bergsma $15.95   0-935699-14-7

"Children's Choice for 1999" by Children's Book Council

Alive with dolphins, parrots and fairies, this magical tale inspires us to believe in the power of our dreams.

TO SLEEP WITH THE ANGELS

By H. Elizabeth Collins, illustrated by Judy Kuusisto $15.95   0-935699-16-3

Finalist – 2000 Visionary Award for Best Children's Book – Coalition of Visionary Retailers

A young girl's guardian Angel comforts her to sleep, filling her dreams with magical adventures.

Direct U.S. Orders: add $2.00 postage; each additional book add $1.00. WA residents add 8.6% sales tax.

ILLUMINATION ARTS PUBLISHING COMPANY

P.O. Box 1865, Bellevue, WA 98009 ✧ 1.888.210.8216 ✧ 425.644.7185 ✧ fax: 425.644.9274
E-mail: liteinfo@illumin.com ✧ www.illumin.com